# HENRY
## AND THE HURRICANE

A BEAR CALLED HENRY STORY

WRITTEN BY **JANIE BURK**
ILLUSTRATED BY **HEATHER DICKINSON**

Dedicated to BRYAN for staying with me on this project
and helping me to see clearly.

Dedicated to BREE for encouraging
and believing in me.

Title: Henry and the Hurricane – First Edition / Janie Burk, author
Heather Dickinson, illustrator

Library of Congress Cataloging-in-Publication Data is on file.
Identifiers: LCCN 2021912537
Paperback ISBN: 978-1-7374-6201-9
Hardcover ISBN: 978-1-7374-6200-2
Published in United States

Written by Janie Burk,  www.janieburk.com
Illustrated by Heather Dickinson, www.heatherdickinson.com

# AUTHOR'S NOTE

It is a delightful thing to read with a child. It is an opportunity to bond and teach as you and your little one share a story. Is this not a great way to spend time together?

A few items related to our story:

1. Our hurricane takes place in the Yucatán Peninsula at the southern tip of Mexico. The peninsula separates the Gulf of Mexico to the west from the Caribbean Sea to the east. The climate here is tropical. Hurricanes and other tropical storms are not uncommon.

2. Page 14: The Yucatán is home to cenotes. These are special pools of water, naturally occurring sinkholes, that form when limestone erodes and the ground collapses. Groundwater fills the hole, and forms a large pool of clear, clean, emerald green to blue appearing water. Cenotes were an important source of water for the ancient Maya people of Yucatán. Today cenotes provide lovely sights and places for people to swim. They are usually associated with large rock formations and are often enclosed in caves.

3. Page 20: Zoo animals eat meat, fruits, vegetables and eggs. Because coconut bearing palm trees grow well in the Yucatán, I added coconut milk as a beverage for the animals. While in Mexico, I learned to drink coconut milk from the whole coconut with one end cut off, and a straw inserted, making this a fun drink.

4. Translations from Spanish to English:
   a. Page 10: "¡Hola! Por favor, ayudenme!" → "Hello! Please, help me."
   b. Page 10: " Sí, por favor." → "Yes, please."
   c. Page 11: "¡Si, las luciernagas!" → "Yes, fireflies!"
   d. Page 26: Tigres → Tigers
   e. Page 27: Monos → Monkeys
   f. Page 30: "Amigos, nos vemos mas tarde," → "My friends, we will see you later."

5. Take-home messages from the story:
   a. There are solutions to our problems.
   b. When we work together for good, good things happen.
   c. When we help others, we are happy.
   d. There are positive ways to view situations. As we look on the positive, we are happier.

*Janie Burk*

Henry the bear and
Juniper the butterfly
come from faraway Bearland
past the mountains and
behind the clouds.

Now they live with Rebekah
and her family.

"This is the best tree in the whole world!"
Henry and Rebekah giggle as they say the same thing.

Juniper is Henry's butterfly.
She flutters down and whispers in Henry's ear.

"There's trouble in Mexico.
A hurricane is coming!"
Henry tells Rebekah.
"No one has let the animals
out of the zoo.
They need our help."

"Mexico is far away. If we want to help
we need to leave soon, and we need to fly."

Juniper makes Rebekah a special cape.
Henry puts the cape on Rebekah and tells her,
"When you wear this you can fly, but it will only work
if you are going to help someone."

Henry, Rebekah and Juniper fly to the zoo in Mexico.

When they arrive, Henry and Rebekah see the zoo animals
running back and forth making loud noises.
"They are afraid," says Henry.

The zookeeper is afraid too.
"¡Hola! ¡Por favor, ayudenme! I am Señor Garcia.
A big storm is coming. The animals need shelter."
"We will find a place," says Henry.
"Sí, por favor. My son, Miguel, can help you,
and I will get the animals ready to leave quickly."

Miguel climbs onto Henry's back, and Henry, Rebekah and Miguel fly away to look for a place for the animals.

Miguel sees a cave. "Look!" he cries.
They stop to look. It's dark inside.
"We need light," says Rebekah.
"I know who can help," replies Henry. "Fireflies!"
"¡Sí, las luciernagas! I can show you where they live,"
says Miguel.

Henry asks the fireflies for help.

The fireflies agree to follow Henry.

Together they go into the cave. The fireflies glow, and Henry, Rebekah and Miguel see a large pool of water.

"What is this?" asks Rebekah.
"This is a cenote," replies Miguel. "It happens when
a big hole in the ground fills with water."
"We can stay here during the storm," says Henry.
"Let's get Señor Garcia and the animals."

They all go to the cenote.

Inside there is room for everyone.

Outside the wind blows hard. It knocks coconuts off of trees and thatched roofs off of huts.

Henry brings coconuts, and the animals bring a thatched roof to the cave. Henry and the animals cover the entrance to keep the storm from coming in.

Outside the wind whooshes. Rain beats on the ground. Branches snap off trees.

Inside it is calm and dry, but some of the animals are still afraid. Señor Garcia shows Henry, Rebekah and Miguel how to comfort them. Henry and the children stay with the animals. They scratch ears and rub bellies until the animals feel better.

Before long the monkeys start to tumble around.
The kangaroos jump rope.

The hippos dance on tiptoes.
The animals laugh and play.
Some swim, and some drink
coconut milk.

After much fun, the animals snuggle together and go to sleep.

The next morning there is no whooshing wind,
beating rain or clattering branches.
Henry lifts the roof from the cenote, and they go out.

The sky is blue. The sun is up. The storm has passed.
The animals stretch and shake and nibble wet grass.

Soon they return to the zoo. It is a mess!

Cages are broken. Trees are tangled with benches. Bushes are mixed up with broken signs.

Everyone pitches in to clean up and set things right.
Henry whistles, and the animals sing.

The zoo is happy and noisy.
The animals are glad to be home.

It is time for Henry and Rebekah to leave.
Everyone gathers together.

"Amigos, nos vemos mas tarde," the animals say.
"Yes, we will see you later," reply Henry and Rebekah.

The animals, Henry and Rebekah are happy
with their new friends.

And until they see these new friends again,
they will be happy with their old friends.

Lightning Source UK Ltd.
Milton Keynes UK
UKHW051303010821
387983UK00002B/110